📖 TIMELESS SHAKESPEARE

MACBETH
William Shakespeare

– ADAPTED BY –

Brady Timoney

SADDLEBACK
EDUCATIONAL PUBLISHING

TIMELESS SHAKESPEARE

Hamlet

Julius Caesar

King Lear

Macbeth

The Merchant of Venice

A Midsummer Night's Dream

Othello

Romeo and Juliet

The Tempest

Twelfth Night

SADDLEBACK
EDUCATIONAL PUBLISHING
www.sdlback.com

ISBN-13: 978-1-61651-105-0
ISBN-10: 1-61651-105-2
eBook: 978-1-60291-839-9

Printed in the Malaysia

21 20 19 18 17   9 10 11 12 13

| Contents |

– INTRODUCTION –

In the year 1040, Macbeth and Banquo, two victorious generals, meet three mysterious witches on a heath in Scotland. The witches predict that Macbeth will one day be King of Scotland. They tell Banquo that his sons will also sit on the throne. Urged on by his wife, Macbeth kills King Duncan and is declared king. Fearing the second part of the witches' prophecy, Macbeth has Banquo killed. When Duncan's son Malcolm raises an army to oppose Macbeth, Lady Macbeth, tormented by guilt, commits suicide. Macbeth is then killed by Macduff, and Malcolm is crowned king.

– CAST OF CHARACTERS –

DUNCAN King of Scotland

MALCOLM and **DONALBAIN** His sons

MACBETH General in the king's army

BANQUO General in the king's army

LENNOX, ROSS, MACDUFF, ANGUS, CAITHNESS, MENTEITH Noblemen of Scotland

FLEANCE Son of Banquo

SIWARD Earl of Northumberland, General of the English Forces

YOUNG SIWARD His son

SEYTON An officer attending on Macbeth

BOY Son to Macduff

An **ENGLISH DOCTOR**, a **SCOTTISH DOCTOR**, a **SOLDIER**, a **PORTER**, an **OLD MAN**

LADY MACBETH

LADY MACDUFF Gentlewoman attending on Lady Macbeth

THREE WITCHES

LORDS, GENTLEMEN, OFFICERS, SOLDIERS, MURDERERS, ATTENDANTS, and **MESSENGERS**

The **GHOST OF BANQUO** and **SEVERAL OTHER APPARITIONS**

ACT 1

Scene 1

*(An open place. Thunder and lightning. **Three witches** enter.)*

WITCH 1: When shall we three meet again?
  In thunder, in lightning, or in rain?

WITCH 2: When the hurlyburly's done,
  When the battle's lost and won.

WITCH 3: Before the setting of the sun.

WITCH 1: Where shall we meet?

WITCH 2: On the heath.

WITCH 3: There we will meet with Macbeth.

WITCH 1: Let's go home for now.

ALL: Fair is foul, and foul is fair—
  Fly through the fog and filthy air.

*(The **witches** vanish.)*

Scene 2

*(A camp near Forres. Alarms are heard offstage. **King Duncan, Malcolm, Donalbain**, and **Lennox** enter, with **attendants**. They meet a bleeding **soldier**.)*

DUNCAN: What bloody man is that?
  From the way he looks, he can tell us
  How the battle is going.

MALCOLM: This is the man
  Who fought against my capture.
  (to the soldier): Hail, brave friend!
  How is the battle going?

SOLDIER: Macbeth's sword smoked as he
  Carved out his passage through the battle!
  Finally he faced the villain Macdonald.
  He didn't shake hands or say farewell.
  Instead, he cut him from belly to jaws
  And placed his head high on the castle
    walls.

DUNCAN: Oh, brave and worthy cousin!

SOLDIER: Then problems came from the east.
  Listen, King of Scotland, listen!
  When the rebels started to run, the
  Norwegian lord saw an advantage.
  With fresh arms and new supplies of men,
  He launched a new attack.

DUNCAN: Didn't this dismay
  Our captains, Macbeth and Banquo?

SOLDIER: Yes—like a sparrow dismays an eagle
  Or a hare dismays a lion!
  They were, my king,
  Like cannons with double charges!
  For each stroke by the enemy,

They gave back two.
But I am faint. My wounds cry out!

DUNCAN: Your words and your wounds
Both tell of your honor.
(to the attendants): Go, get him doctors.

*(The **soldier** exits, with **attendants**.)*

(to Malcolm): Who comes here?

MALCOLM: The worthy thane of Ross.

*(**Ross** enters.)*

ROSS: God save the king!

DUNCAN: Where were you, worthy thane?

ROSS: In Fife, great king,
Where Norwegian flags fill the sky
And chill our people with fear.
The King of Norway himself, leading
many men, began a battle.
He was helped by that most disloyal
traitor, the Thane of Cawdor.
At last, Macbeth, dressed in armor,
Challenged him with greater strength.
Point for point, arm against arm,
Macbeth wore him down. In the end,
The victory fell on us.

DUNCAN: Great happiness!

ROSS: Now, Sweno, Norway's king,
Wants to surrender.

We forbade him to bury his men
Until he paid us $10,000.

DUNCAN: Never again shall the
Thane of Cawdor betray us!
Go see to his instant death,
And greet Macbeth with his former title.

ROSS: I'll see it done.

DUNCAN: What he has lost, noble Macbeth has
won.

*(**All** exit.)*

| Scene 3 |

*(A heath near Forres. Thunder. The **three witches**
enter. A drum is heard offstage.)*

WITCH 1: A drum, a drum!
Macbeth does come.

ALL: The weird sisters, hand in hand,
Travelers over sea and land,
Thus do go about, about.
Three times to yours, three times to mine,
And three times again, to make up nine.
That's it! The charm's wound up.

*(**Macbeth** and **Banquo** enter.)*

MACBETH: So foul and fair a day I have not
seen.

BANQUO: How far is it to Forres?
   (He sees the witches.) What are these
      creatures, so withered
   And so wild in their clothing?
   They do not look like inhabitants
   Of the earth, and yet they are on it.

MACBETH: Speak, if you can. What are you?

WITCH 1: Hail, Macbeth, Thane of Glamis!

WITCH 2: Hail, Macbeth, Thane of Cawdor!

WITCH 3: Hail, Macbeth, who shall be king
      hereafter!

BANQUO: Why do you draw back, Macbeth?
   Why fear what sounds so fair?
   (to the witches): In the name of truth,
   Are you fantasies, or are you indeed
   What you seem to be? You greet
   My noble partner with fair predictions
   About his future. You say he will have
   Noble possessions and royal rank.
   Why do you not speak to me?
   If you can look into the seeds of time,
   And say which grain will grow,
   And which will not,
   Speak then to me, who neither begs nor
      fears your favors nor your hate.

WITCH 1: Hail!

WITCH 2: Hail!

WITCH 3: Hail!

WITCH 1: Lesser than Macbeth, and greater.

WITCH 2: Not so happy, yet much happier.

WITCH 3: Your sons and grandsons shall
Be kings, though you will not.
So all hail, Macbeth and Banquo!

WITCH 1: Banquo and Macbeth, all hail!

MACBETH: Tell me more. Since my father's
death,
I have been Thane of Glamis.
But how can I be Thane of Cawdor, too?
The Thane of Cawdor is still alive,
A well-to-do gentleman. And to be king
Is no more possible than to be
Thane of Cawdor. Say from where
You got this strange information.
And why have you stopped us on this
godforsaken heath
With such greetings and prophecies?
Speak, I say!

*(**Witches** vanish.)*

BANQUO: Earth has bubbles, as water does,
And these must be bubbles, too.
Look! They have vanished!

MACBETH: Into the air,
What seemed real has melted
As breath into the wind.
I wish they had stayed!

BANQUO: Were they really here?
　Or has some food we've eaten
　Taken our reason prisoner?

MACBETH: Your children shall be kings.

BANQUO: *You* shall be king!

MACBETH: And Thane of Cawdor, too.
　Isn't that what they said?

BANQUO: Yes. They used those very words.
　(hearing a sound) Who's there?

***(Ross** and **Angus** enter.)*

ROSS: The king has happily received
　The news of your success, Macbeth!
　He was astonished
　When he heard of your brave deeds
　In the battle against the rebels.
　All reports proclaimed your praises
　In his kingdom's great defense.
　The king is very pleased to hear
　Of your fearlessness during battle.

ANGUS: As advance payment
　Toward an even greater honor, the king
　Told me to call you Thane of Cawdor.
　So I say, hail, most worthy thane!
　The title is yours.

BANQUO: Those witches told the truth?

MACBETH: But the Thane of Cawdor lives!
　Why do you dress me in borrowed robes?

ANGUS: He who *was* the thane still lives.
But he deserves to lose his life.
He might have actually fought for
  Norway.
Or he might have helped the King of
  Norway in hidden ways.
Perhaps he did both of these things
To work for the ruin of his own country.
I do not know exactly how he did it.
But the charges have been proven,
And he has confessed to treason.
The death sentence has been pronounced.

MACBETH *(aside)*: Thane of Glamis, and now
Thane of Cawdor, too!
And the greatest title is yet to come!
(to Banquo): Do you not hope your children
Shall be kings? After all, those who told me
That I would be the Thane of Cawdor
Promised no less to them.

BANQUO: If we trusted those promises fully,
You might be king as well.
But it is strange. Often, to bring harm to us,
The devil tells us small truths,
Winning us over with small things,
Only to betray us in important things.
(to Ross and Angus): Cousins, a word with
  you, please.

MACBETH *(aside)*: Two of their predictions

Have come true! They seem like happy hints
To the greater prophecy that I will be king.
(to Ross and Angus): I thank you, gentlemen.
(aside): This supernatural prophecy
Might be evil or good. If evil,
Why has it given me evidence of success,
By starting with a truth? For it is true
That I am Thane of Cawdor.
If good, why are horrid thoughts
Making my heart knock at my ribs?
Imagined horrors are worse than real fears.
My thoughts about murdering the king
Shake me until I feel smothered.
Yet nothing else seems real to me.

BANQUO *(to Ross and Angus)*: Look at Macbeth.
He seems to be in a trance.

MACBETH *(aside)*: If my fate is to be king,
Then fate may crown me—
Even if I do nothing.

BANQUO *(to Ross and Angus)*: New honors come
upon Macbeth.
Like new clothes, they do not fit well
Until they've been used for a while.

MACBETH *(aside)*: Come what may,
Time and the hour runs through the
roughest day.

BANQUO: Worthy Macbeth, we're waiting.

MACBETH: Please forgive me.
My thoughts were wandering.
Let us go to meet the king.
(to Banquo): Think about what has happened.
Later, after we've considered things,
Let us speak freely about it.

BANQUO: Very gladly.

MACBETH: Until then, enough! Come, friends.

*(**All** exit.)*

| Scene 4 |

*(Forres. The palace. **King Duncan, Malcolm, Donalbain, Lennox**, and **attendants** enter.)*

DUNCAN: Has the Thane of Cawdor been
executed?
Have the officers returned yet?

MALCOLM: Not yet, my lord. But I have
Spoken with one who saw Cawdor die.
After confessing his treasons,
He begged your highness's pardon.
Nothing in his life
Was as honorable as his leaving it.
He died as one who had rehearsed
Throwing away the dearest thing he
owned
As if it were a careless trifle.

DUNCAN: Alas! There's no way
To read a man's mind in his face!
He was a gentleman in whom I placed
An absolute trust.

(Macbeth, Banquo, Ross, and Angus enter.)

(to Macbeth): Oh, most worthy cousin!
I owe you more than I can ever pay.

MACBETH: Serving you loyally
Is payment in itself. Your highness's role
Is to receive our services. Our duties
Are to do what we can to keep you safe.

DUNCAN: I have only begun to honor you.
Now I will work to see you prosper.
You, noble Banquo, you have deserved
No less. Let me embrace you
And hold you to my heart.

BANQUO: It is an honor to serve you, my lord.

DUNCAN: Sons, kinsmen, thanes,
And all you who are near to me, know this:
I appoint my eldest son, Malcolm,
    as my successor. From now on,
He will be called the Prince of
    Cumberland.
He is not the only one who will be honored.
Signs of nobility, like stars, shall shine
On all those who merit them.
Let us now go to Inverness
To visit Macbeth's castle.

15

MACBETH: I'll go on ahead and tell my wife
 The joyful news of your approach.
 (bowing) I humbly take my leave.

DUNCAN: My worthy Thane of Cawdor!

MACBETH *(aside)*: The Prince of Cumberland!
 That is an obstacle,
 On which I must fall down, or leap over—
 For it lies in my way. Stars, hide your fires!
 Let no light see my black and deep desires.

*(**Macbeth** exits.)*

DUNCAN: True, worthy Banquo!
 I am fed on Macbeth's praises.
 They are a banquet to me. Let us follow
 Him who prospers to bid us welcome.
 He is a kinsman without equal!

*(**All** exit.)*

| Scene 5 |

*(Inverness, Macbeth's castle. **Lady Macbeth** enters, carrying a letter.)*

LADY MACBETH *(reading the letter)*: "The three
 witches proved they can predict the
 future. After they vanished into the air,
 some messengers came from the king.
 They called me 'Thane of Cawdor'—the

same title the weird sisters called me! The witches had also said, 'All hail, Macbeth, who shall be king hereafter!' I thought it good to tell you of this, my dearest partner in greatness. Lose no time in rejoicing over the greatness that is promised! Keep this to yourself, and farewell."

(commenting on the letter): You were already Thane of Glamis, and now Thane of
  Cawdor.
You shall also be what you were promised.
Yet I do fear your nature.
It is too full of the milk of human kindness
To go the fastest way. You yearn to be great.
You have ambition. But your nature lacks
  the necessary ruthlessness.
What you deeply desire
You would attain through honest means.
You would not do anything dishonest
To get it. You need someone
To say, "You must do this, if you want that."
Hurry home, so I may pour my spirit
Into your ear! Let me push you,
With the strength of my own voice,
To overcome all that stands between you
And the golden crown.
Fate and the supernatural have already
Destined you for greatness.

*(A **servant** enters.)*

LADY MACBETH: What is your news?

SERVANT: The king comes here tonight.

LADY MACBETH: You are mad to say it!
Isn't my husband with him? If it were so,
He would have told me to prepare for it.

SERVANT: May it please you, it is true.
Our thane is coming. The messenger
Who brought the news was so weary
From running, he had only enough
Breath to deliver the message.

LADY MACBETH: Take care of him.
He brings great news.

(Servant exits.)

The raven himself is hoarse
From croaking the news of Duncan's fatal
    entrance.
Come, you spirits,
Fill me, from head to toe, full
Of the worst cruelty! Make my blood thick.
Kill any feelings of remorse and sorrow
So that no tender female feelings
May shake my evil purpose.
Come, thick night!
Wrap yourself in the darkest smoke of hell
So my keen knife will not see
The wound it makes, nor will heaven
Peep through the blanket of the dark
To cry, "Stop, stop!"

*(**Macbeth** enters.)*

    Great Glamis! Worthy Cawdor!
    Greater than both, in the near future!
    Your letter has carried me beyond
    The ignorant present! I can feel
    The future in this very instant!

MACBETH: My dearest love,
    Duncan arrives tonight.

LADY MACBETH: And when does he leave?

MACBETH: Tomorrow, or so he plans.

LADY MACBETH: Oh, never
    Shall he see the sun again!
    Your face, my thane, is like a book
    Where anyone can read strange things.
    To fool the time, look like the time.
    Show welcome in your eye,
    Your hand, your words.
    Look like the innocent flower
    But be the serpent under it.
    He who is coming must be provided for.
    You shall put this night's great business
    In my hands. I will take care of
      everything!
    Then all our nights and days to come
    Will be spent as king and queen.

MACBETH: We will speak further.

LADY MACBETH: Just remain calm.

Do nothing that looks suspicious.
Leave all the rest to me.

(Both *exit.)*

| Scene 6 |

(Before Macbeth's castle. **King Duncan, Malcolm,
Donalbain, Banquo, Lennox, Macduff, Ross, Angus,**
and **servants** *enter.)*

DUNCAN: This castle is in a pleasant place.
The air softly and sweetly appeals
To our gentle senses.

BANQUO *(pointing to a bird)***:** These birds often
Make their nests where the air is delicate.

(Lady Macbeth *enters.)*

DUNCAN: See, see, our honored hostess!
I thank you for the trouble you take
In preparing for our visit.

LADY MACBETH: Had we done twice as much,
And then twice that much again,
It would not equal the deep honor
Which your majesty brings to our house.

DUNCAN: Give me your hand, and show me
To my beloved host.

(All *exit.)*

| Scene 7 |

*(Within Macbeth's castle. **Macbeth** enters.)*

MACBETH: If it must be done,
Then it's best done quickly.
If only the assassination could end it!
Followed by success, that would be fine.
But we still face judgment. This justice
Makes us think twice about such evil.
Duncan's here in double trust—
First, I am his kinsman and his subject.
This argues strongly against the deed.
Second, I am his host.
I should shut the door against his
    murderer,
Not bear the knife myself! Besides,
Duncan is a good man. His virtues
Plead like angels against his murder.
I have no good reason to do this,
Except my own ambition, which, like an
    eager rider, may jump over the horse,
And fall on the other side.

*(**Lady Macbeth** enters.)*

What news?

LADY MACBETH: He is almost finished supper.
Why have you left the room?

MACBETH: Has he asked for me?

LADY MACBETH: Don't you know he has?

MACBETH: We will go no further with the plan.
He has honored me, and I have earned
Golden opinions from all sorts of people.
I should wear these now while they are new
And not cast them aside so soon.

LADY MACBETH: What about your hopes
For the future? Have they been sleeping?
Are you afraid to be the same in your act
As you are in your desire? Would you
Live as a coward in your own eyes,
Saying "I dare not" rather than "I will"?
You are like the cat who wanted the fish
But was afraid to get its paws wet.

MACBETH: I beg you, be quiet!
I dare do all that a man may do.
Who dares to do more is not a man.

LADY MACBETH (angrily): What beast was it, then,
That made you talk about this plan to me?
When you dared to do it, you were a man.
To be *more* than you were,
You would be so much more the man.
Come now—you have sworn to do it!

MACBETH: What if we should fail?

LADY MACBETH: With enough courage, we'll not
fail. When Duncan is asleep,
I'll give his two guards wine and liquor.
They'll soon be asleep, too.

We'll kill the unguarded Duncan.
It will be easy
To blame his drunken guards, who
Shall bear the guilt of our great murder.

MACBETH: Yes! After we have marked with
Duncan's blood
Those two sleeping guards,
And used their very daggers for the crime,
Everyone will think they did it.

LADY MACBETH: Who could think otherwise—
Especially when we'll be crying the loudest
About his death?

MACBETH: Then it's settled.
Away, and fool the time with fairest show.
False face must hide what false heart does
know.

(They exit.)

Act 2

| Scene 1 |

*(The courtyard of Macbeth's castle. **Banquo, Fleance**, and a **servant** carrying a torch enter.)*

BANQUO: What time is it, son?

SERVANT: After midnight, sir.

BANQUO: There is thriftiness in the heavens,
For the stars, like candles, are all out.
A heavy feeling lies on me like lead,
And yet I could not sleep. Merciful
Powers, hold back my cursed thoughts
That keep me from sleeping!
(hearing a noise): Who's there?

*(**Macbeth** and a **servant** carrying a torch enter.)*

MACBETH: A friend.

BANQUO: What, sir, not asleep yet?
The king's in bed. He was in a good
   mood
And sent great gifts to your officers.
He said your wife is a wonderful hostess,
And then he retired, very content.

MACBETH: Being unprepared for his visit,
I fear that we didn't do enough for him.

BANQUO: All was well. I dreamed last night

Of the three weird sisters.
For you, their first prediction has come true!

MACBETH: If you are loyal to me, honors
shall be yours when the time comes.

BANQUO: I lose no honor in seeking to add to
it. If I can keep my conscience
Free while staying loyal, then, of course,
I shall take your advice.

MACBETH: Sleep well, then!

BANQUO: Thank you, sir. The same to you!

*(**Banquo**, **Fleance**, and their **servant** exit.)*

MACBETH *(to his servant)*: Tell my wife to
Strike the bell when my drink is ready.

*(**Servant** exits.)*

Is this a dagger I seem to see before me,
The handle toward my hand?
Are you, fatal vision, able to be felt
As well as seen? Or are you only
A dagger of the mind, a false creation,
Coming from my fevered brain?
I can see you still, in a form as real
As this one, which now I draw.

(He draws out his own, real dagger.)

You show me the way I meant to go.
Are my eyes made fools by my
Other senses, or better than the rest?

I still see you. Your blade has bits of blood
That were not there before. You're not real.
This bloody business makes me see things!
Now half the world is slumbering.
Wicked dreams come to those who sleep.
Sure and firm earth, hear not my steps.
Do not notice which way they walk.
I fear your very stones tell where I am.
While I talk, Duncan still lives.
Words blow cold air on the heat of deeds.

(A bell rings.)

I go, and it is done. The bell invites me.
Hear it not, Duncan, for it calls from
Your grave in the cold ground.

*(**Macbeth** exits. **Lady Macbeth** enters.)*

LADY MACBETH: That which made them drunk
Has made me bold. What quenched
Their thirst has set me afire. Listen!
The owl shrieks, the fatal bellman
Which says the last good night.
Ah! I see the drunken guards
Mock their king with snores. I have drugged
Their drinks, so that death and nature
Fight over them, whether they live or die.

MACBETH *(offstage)***:** What's going on?

LADY MACBETH *(to herself)***:** Alas! They've
awakened,

And it is not done yet. The attempt,
And not the deed, ruins us!
I put their daggers out in plain sight.
He could not miss them. If Duncan had
Not looked like my own father in his
  sleep, I would have done it myself.

(Macbeth *enters again, covered with blood.)*

LADY MACBETH: My husband!

MACBETH: I have done the deed.
  Did you not hear a noise?

LADY MACBETH: I heard the owl scream
  And the crickets cry.

MACBETH: One man laughed in his sleep.
Another one cried, "Murder!"
They seemed to wake each other up,
But quickly went back to sleep.

LADY MACBETH: Two guests are sleeping in a
room near Duncan's.

MACBETH: One cried, "God bless us!"
The other said, "Amen."
I feared that they had seen me
With these bloody hands.
Hearing their fear, I could not say, "Amen"
When they said, "God bless us!"

LADY MACBETH: Your thoughts are too deep.

MACBETH: But why could I not say, "Amen"?
I had most need of blessing,
And "Amen" stuck in my throat.

LADY MACBETH: We must not dwell on these
deeds, or we will go mad.

MACBETH: I heard a voice cry, "Sleep no more!
Macbeth does murder sleep!"
Only the innocent sleep—sleep that
Knits up the raveled sleeve of care,
The death of each day's worries,
Medicine for hurt minds,
The greatest nourisher in life's feast.

LADY MACBETH: What do you mean?

MACBETH: Still it cried, "Sleep no more!"

To all the house. "Glamis has murdered sleep,
And therefore Cawdor shall sleep no more.
Macbeth shall sleep no more!"

LADY MACBETH: Who cried this out, worthy thane?
You are wasting your noble strength
Thinking such foolish thoughts. Go wash
This filthy evidence from your hands.
Why did you bring these daggers with you?
They must lie there. Go, take them back!
Smear the sleeping guards with blood!

MACBETH: I can't go back. I'm afraid to look
upon what I have done!

LADY MACBETH: Coward! I'll take the daggers.
The sleeping and the dead are but pictures
Of each other. Only a child would fear them!
I'll paint the guards' faces with his blood
To make them look guilty.

(She exits. A knocking is heard.)

MACBETH: What is that knocking?
Why does every noise frighten me?
What hands are these?
Will all the ocean wash away this blood?
My hands could make the green seas red!

(Lady Macbeth enters again.)

LADY MACBETH: My hands are of your color,
But I am ashamed to wear a heart so white.

29

(more knocking)

LADY MACBETH: I hear knocking at the south entry.
Let's go to our chamber and wash our hands.
How easy it is then!

(more knocking)

Listen! More knocking.
Get on your nightclothes. We must look
As if we've been sleeping. Don't be lost
So poorly in your thoughts.

MACBETH: I'd rather be lost in thought than
Have to look at my deed.

(more knocking)

Wake Duncan with your knocking! I wish
you could!

*(**Both** exit. A **porter** enters. More knocking.)*

PORTER: Who's knocking? I'm coming!

*(He opens the gate. **Macduff and Lennox** enter.)*

MACDUFF: Is your master awake? Oh, I see that
Our knocking waked him. Here he comes.

*(**Macbeth** enters, wearing nightclothes.)*

LENNOX: Good morning, noble sir!

MACBETH: Good morning, both of you!

MACDUFF: Is the king awake, worthy thane?

MACBETH: Not yet, I think.

MACDUFF: He told me to call on him early.
I've almost missed the time he requested.

MACBETH: There's the door to his chamber.

(Macduff exits.)

LENNOX: Is the king leaving today?

MACBETH: Yes. At least, that's what he said.

LENNOX: The night has been wild. Where we
Were sleeping, our chimneys blew down.
And they say there was wailing heard,
Strange screams of death, and
Terrible predictions of fire and confusion.
The owl shrieked all night.
Some say the feverish earth was shaking!

MACBETH: It was a rough night.

LENNOX: I cannot remember another like it.

(Macduff enters again.)

MACDUFF *(upset)***:** Oh, horror, horror, horror!
Neither tongue nor heart
Can imagine or name it!

MACBETH AND LENNOX: What's the matter?

MACDUFF: Confusion has made its masterpiece!
A most unholy murder has broken open
The lord's holy temple, and stolen from it
The life of the building.

MACBETH: What is it you say—the life?

31

LENNOX: Do you mean his majesty?

MACDUFF: Approach his room,
And destroy your sight by looking.
Do not ask me to speak!
See, and then speak yourselves.

*(**Macbeth** and **Lennox** exit.)*

Awake, awake!
Ring the alarm bell! Murder and treason!
Banquo and Donalbain! Malcolm! Awake!
Shake off this gentle sleep, death's copy,
And look on death itself! Up, up, and see
The sight of the great doom!
Malcolm! Banquo!
Rise up to see this horror!

*(Alarm bell rings. **Lady Macbeth** enters again.)*

LADY MACBETH: What's all this?
Why such a terrible noise
To wake the sleepers of this house? Speak!

MACDUFF: Oh, gentle lady,
It is not for you to hear my words.
To repeat them in a woman's ear
Would murder her as the words were said.

*(**Banquo** enters again.)*

Oh, Banquo, Banquo!
Our royal master has been murdered!

LADY MACBETH: Woe, alas! In our house?

BANQUO: It would be too cruel anywhere.
Dear Macduff, I beg you, say it is not so.

(Macbeth, Lennox, and Ross enter.)

MACBETH: If only I had died an hour ago,
I would have lived a blessed time.
Now there's nothing serious in life.
All is but toys. Honor and grace are dead.
The wine of life has been poured.
Only the dregs are left.

(Malcolm and Donalbain enter.)

DONALBAIN: What is wrong?

MACBETH: You are—and you do not know it.
The spring, the fountain of your blood,
Is stopped. The very source of it is stopped.

MACDUFF: Your royal father is murdered.

MALCOLM: Oh, no! By whom?

LENNOX: It seems that his own guards did it.
Their hands and faces were covered in blood.
So were their daggers, which we found,
Unwiped, on their pillows.
No man's life was to be trusted with them.

MACBETH: Even so, I am sorry for the fury
That made me kill them.

MACDUFF: Why did you do it, then?

MACBETH: Who can be wise and confused,
Calm and furious, loyal and neutral,

All at once? No man. My love for Duncan
Outran my reason. Here lay our king,
His silver skin laced with his golden blood.
There were the murderers, covered in
Duncan's blood, their daggers
Smeared with gore! Anyone who
Had a heart to love, and in that heart
Courage to make that love known,
Would have done the same.

LADY MACBETH *(fainting)*: Help me!

MACDUFF: Look after the lady.

MALCOLM *(aside to Donalbain)*: Why do we
Hold our tongues, while everyone else
Talks about this subject so important to us?

DONALBAIN *(aside to Malcolm)*: We are not safe.
Our fate might be hiding
In some secret place, ready to rush out
And seize us. Let's get away.
We can cry over our father's death later.

BANQUO: Look after the lady.

(Lady Macbeth is carried out.)

Let's all go and get dressed.
Then let us meet here later to talk about
This most bloody piece of work
And try to learn more about it.
Fears and doubts shake us.
In the great hand of God I stand,

And from there, I will fight
Against the unknown forces of
Treason and evil.

MACDUFF: And so will I.

ALL: And so will we all.

MACBETH: Let's put on our armor,
And meet together in the hall.

*(**All** but Malcolm and Donalbain exit.)*

MALCOLM: What will you do?
Let's not meet with the others.
Showing an unfelt sorrow is something
That false men do easily. I will go to
England.

DONALBAIN: And I'll go to Ireland.
We'll be safer if we are separated.
Where we are now, there are daggers
In men's smiles. Our closest relations
Are the most likely to kill us.

MALCOLM: The murderous arrow
That's been shot has not yet landed.
Our safest course is to avoid the aim.
Let us not say goodbye to anyone,
But secretly steal away. There's no honor
Where there's no mercy left.

*(**Malcolm** and **Donalbain** exit.)*

| Scene 2 |

*(Outside Macbeth's castle. **Ross** and **Macduff** enter.)*

ROSS: Is it known who did this bloody deed?

MACDUFF: The guards that Macbeth killed.

ROSS: But what was their motive?

MACDUFF: They were hired by someone.
  Malcolm and Donalbain, the king's sons,
  Have run away. This makes them look
    guilty to the thanes.

ROSS: An act against nature! Why would
  They want to kill their own father?
  Now it is most likely that the crown will
  Pass on to Macbeth.

MACDUFF: He has already been named king.
  He has gone to Scone to be crowned.

ROSS: Where is Duncan's body?

MACDUFF: It's been carried to Scone,
  To the sacred tomb of Scottish kings.

ROSS: Will you go to Scone?

MACDUFF: No, cousin. I'll go home, to Fife.

ROSS: Well, I'll go to Scone.

MACDUFF: May you see things well-done there.
  Farewell!

ROSS: And farewell to you.

*(**Ross** and **Macduff** exit.)*

Act 3

| Scene 1 |

*(Forres. A room in the palace. **Banquo** enters.)*

BANQUO *(to himself)***:** You have it now—
King, Cawdor, Glamis—
All that the weird sisters promised.
If they told the truth about you,
Perhaps they told the truth about me
As well. If so, I have strong hopes.
But hush, no more.

*(Trumpets sound. **Macbeth** enters as king, followed by **Lady Macbeth** as queen, **Lennox**, **Ross**, lords, ladies, and **attendants**.)*

MACBETH: A banquet is being held tonight, sir,
And I want you to be there.

BANQUO: Your wish is my command, highness.

MACBETH: Are you going riding this afternoon?

BANQUO: Yes, my good lord.

MACBETH: Will you be riding far?

BANQUO: As far, my lord, as will fill up
The time between now and supper.

MACBETH: Do not fail to come to the feast.

BANQUO: My lord, I will not.

MACBETH: We hear that our bloody cousins,
Malcolm and Donalbain, have gone to
England and to Ireland. They have not
Confessed to killing their father.
Instead, they fill their hearers' ears
With wild stories about his death.
But we'll talk about that tomorrow.
Farewell, until you return at night.
Is Fleance going with you?

BANQUO: Yes, my good lord.

*(**Banquo** exits. Macbeth speaks to the others.)*

MACBETH: You may do whatever you like
Until seven tonight. To make the company
Even sweeter then, we will stay alone this
afternoon. God be with you.

*(**All** exit but Macbeth and a servant.)*

MACBETH *(to the servant.)***:** We sent for some
men. Are they here yet?

SERVANT: Yes, my lord. They are at the gate.

MACBETH: Bring them before us.

*(**Servant** exits.)*

MACBETH: To be king is nothing,
Unless one's position is safe.
Our fears about Banquo run deep.
He threatens my greatness.

When the weird sisters called me king,
They called him father to a line of kings.
Upon my head they placed a fruitless
  crown, to be taken from me one day
By no son of mine.
If the prophecies are true,
I have murdered the gracious Duncan
Just to make Banquo's sons kings!
Rather than that, let fate come to
The battle as my champion.
(He hears a noise.) Who's there?

(Servant *enters again, with* **two murderers**.)

Go to the door until we call.

(Servant *exits.)*

Was it not yesterday we spoke together?

MURDERER 1: It was, your highness.

MACBETH: Well, then, have you considered
What I said? Do you understand
That it was Banquo who was responsible
For your bad fortune in the past, and not
My innocent self, as you had thought?

MURDERER 1: You made it known to us.

MACBETH: Can you forgive? Are you so
Good that you can pray for him
When his heavy hand has ruined you
And made beggars of your own children?

MURDERER 1: We are men, my lord.

MACBETH: Yes, in the list of species,
　　You are described as men,
　　Just as hounds, greyhounds, mongrels,
　　Spaniels, curs, waterdogs, and wolves are
　　All called by the name of dogs.
　　The best kind of list tells the difference
　　Between the swift, the slow, the wild,
　　The housedog, the hunter. Each one has
　　A special gift granted by nature.
　　And so it is with men.
　　Do you rate yourselves above
　　The worst rank of men? Say so,
　　And I will give you a special assignment
　　Which will take your enemy off the list
　　And bring you closer to my affection.
　　For I wear my health sickly while he lives,
　　But with his death, my life will be perfect.

MURDERER 2: My lord, I am one who is
　　So angry at the evil blows of the world
　　That I am reckless about what I do
　　To spite the world.

MURDERER 1: And I am another—so weary
　　With disasters, tugged by bad luck,
　　That I would bet my life on any chance
　　To mend it or be rid of it.

MACBETH: You know Banquo was your enemy.

BOTH MURDERERS: True, my lord.

MACBETH: He is my enemy, too.
Every minute of his being feels like a
Knife thrust to my heart. Though I could
Sweep him from sight with my power,
I must not do so. Certain friends that are
Both his and mine would mourn his fall,
And I need their loyalty.
This is why I ask your help. Do this—
But let no suspicion fall on me!

MURDERER 2: My lord, we shall do as you ask.

MACBETH: It must be done tonight.
And it must be done away from the palace.
Remember that I must not be suspected.
Do not botch this work!
Fleance, Banquo's son, will be with him.
His death is no less important to me
Than his father's. He must face the fate
Of that dark hour. Wait outside the gate.
I'll come to you soon with more
instructions.

*(**Murderers** exit.)*

It is arranged. Banquo, your soul's flight,
If it is to heaven, must find it out tonight.

*(**Macbeth** exits.)*

| Scene 2 |

*(**Lady Macbeth** and a **servant** enter a room in the palace.)*

LADY MACBETH: Tell the king to come to me.

SERVANT: Madam, I will.

*(**Servant** exits.)*

LADY MACBETH: Nothing is ours, all is spent,
When we have our desire but are not content.

*(**Macbeth** enters.)*

My lord! Why look so sad?
Things that cannot be changed
Should be forgotten. What's done is done.

MACBETH: We have cut the snake, not killed it.
She'll heal herself, and then we will
Be in great danger. It would be better
To be with the peaceful dead,
Than to suffer this torture of the mind.
Duncan is in his grave.
After life's fitful fever, he sleeps well.
Treason has done his worst.
Nothing can touch him further.

LADY MACBETH: Come on, my gentle lord.
Sleek over your rugged looks.
Be bright and happy with our guests
tonight.

MACBETH: I shall, my love.

And so, I hope, shall you.
Let your attention be given to Banquo.
Show him honor, both with your eyes
And with your words. For a while yet,
We are unsafe. We must make our faces
Masks to our hearts, disguising them.

LADY MACBETH: You must stop this.

MACBETH: Oh, full of scorpions is my mind,
Dear wife! Banquo and Fleance live.

LADY MACBETH: But they won't live forever.

MACBETH: That's comforting, so be joyful.
Before the bat has flown from its cave
Into the darkness of the night,
A dreadful deed shall be done.

LADY MACBETH: What's to be done?

MACBETH: Be innocent of the knowledge
Until you applaud the deed. Come, night!
Blindfold the tender eye of pitiful day.
With your bloody and invisible hand
Cancel and tear to pieces that great bond
That keeps me pale! Light thickens,
And the crow makes wing to the woods.
The good day begins to droop and drowse,
While night's black agents go to their prey.
You wonder at my words, but you'll see
How evil makes bad things even worse.
So, please, go with me.

(Both exit.)

| Scene 3 |

*(A park near the palace. **Three murderers** enter.)*

MURDERER 1: Who told you to join us?

MURDERER 3: Macbeth.

MURDERER 2 *(to murderer 1)*: We have
No reason to mistrust him.
He gave us our orders.

MURDERER 1: Then stand with us.
The west still glimmers with streaks of day.
The late traveler is hurrying along
To reach an inn before dark.
Soon, those we wait for will approach.

MURDERER 3: Listen! I hear horses.

BANQUO *(offstage)*: Give us a light there!

MURDERER 2: That must be Banquo.
The rest of the dinner guests
Are already in the court.

MURDERER 1: The groom is taking the horses
To the stable. Banquo and Fleance
Will walk to the palace gate.

MURDERER 2: I see a light! A light!

MURDERER 3: They're almost here! Get ready!

*(**Banquo** and **Fleance** enter. Fleance carries a torch.)*

BANQUO: It looks like rain tonight.

MURDERER 1: Let it pour!

(Murderer 1 strikes out the light. The others attack Banquo.)

BANQUO: Oh, treachery! Run, good Fleance!
Run, run, run! Avenge me later! Farewell!

*(Banquo dies. **Fleance** escapes.)*

MURDERER 3: Who struck out the light?

MURDERER 1: Wasn't that the best way?

MURDERER 3: There's only one down.
The son has fled.

MURDERER 2: We have failed
In the most important part of our job!

MURDERER 1: We must go and tell Macbeth.

*(**All** exit.)*

| Scene 4 |

*(The banquet room in the palace. **Macbeth, Lady Macbeth, Ross, Lennox, lords**, and **attendants** enter.)*

MACBETH: Welcome! You know your own ranks.
Sit in your proper places.

LORDS: Thanks to your majesty.

MACBETH: I'll mingle with our guests,
And play the humble host.
Our hostess will welcome you
At the proper time.

LADY MACBETH: Please say it for me, sir.
  Tell all our friends,
  For my heart says they are welcome.

MACBETH *(to Lady Macbeth)***:** See—our guests
  Meet you with their hearts' thanks.
  *(to guests)***:** Both sides of the table are even.
  I will sit in the middle.

*(**Murderer 1** enters and stands near the door.)*

  Enjoy yourselves. Soon we'll have a toast
  To start off the meal.

*(**Macbeth** walks toward the door as the guests talk.
He whispers to murderer 1.)*

  There's blood on your face.

MURDERER 1: It is Banquo's, then.

MACBETH: Better outside you than inside him.
  Is he dead?

MURDERER 1: My lord, his throat is cut.
  That I did for him.

MACBETH: You are the best of the cutthroats.
  Who did the same for Fleance?
  If you did it, you are surely the best.

MURDERER 1: Most royal sir, Fleance escaped.

MACBETH: Oh, no! That's terrible!
  My life would have been perfect,
  As broad and free as the air.
  But now I am confined, bound in
  By doubts and fears. But Banquo's dead?

MURDERER 1: Yes, my good lord.
Dead in a ditch he lies,
With twenty gashes on his head,
The least of which would have killed him.

MACBETH: My thanks for that.
The grown serpent lies dead. The worm
That has fled will soon have venom—
But as yet he has no teeth. Go now.
Tomorrow we'll talk again.

*(**Murderer 1** exits.)*

LADY MACBETH: My royal lord,
You did not give the toast! It's no feast
Without a ceremony. Mere eating is best
Done at home. Away from home,
Ceremony is the sauce to the meat.
A feast is bare without it. Be a good host.
Make your guests feel welcome.

MACBETH: Sweet reminder!
Now, good health to all! Enjoy the feast.

LENNOX: May it please your highness to sit.

*(The **ghost of Banquo**, visible only to **Macbeth**, enters and sits in Macbeth's place. Macbeth does not see it yet.)*

MACBETH: All the noblemen of our country
Would be seated under one roof,
If only Banquo were present. I hope
It is thoughtlessness rather than some
Accident that has made him late.

ROSS: His absence, sir, breaks his promise.
Would it please your highness to be seated?

MACBETH: The table's full.

LENNOX: Here is an empty seat, sir.

MACBETH: Where?

LENNOX: Right here, my good lord.

(Lennox sees that Macbeth seems upset. Macbeth has just set eyes on Banquo's ghost.)

What's wrong, your highness?

MACBETH: Which of you has done this?

LORDS: What, my good lord?

MACBETH *(to ghost)*: You cannot say I did it!
Do not shake your bloody hair at me.

ROSS: Gentlemen, rise. His highness is ill.

LADY MACBETH: Sit, worthy friends.
My lord is often like this, and has been
Since his youth. Please, stay seated.
The fit is temporary. In a moment,
He will again be well. If you stare,
You will offend him and make it worse.
Eat, and pay no attention to him.
(aside, to Macbeth): Are you a man?

MACBETH: Yes, and a bold one, who dares
Look on that which might scare the devil.

LADY MACBETH *(aside to Macbeth)*: Nonsense!
What are you afraid of? Shame on you!

Why do you make such faces? In the end,
You're only looking at a stool.

MACBETH: No, see there? Behold! Look!
Can't you see it?
(to the ghost): Why, what do I care?
If you cannot nod, you cannot speak, either.
Do our graves send back those we bury?
Maybe we should feed our dead to the birds.

*(**Ghost** disappears.)*

LADY MACBETH *(aside to Macbeth):* Shame!

MACBETH: As I am standing here, I saw him.
Blood has been shed before now.
Yes, and murders have been performed

That are too terrible to hear about.
In the past, when the brains were hit,
The man would die, and that would end it.
But now they rise again,
And push us from our stools.
This is much stranger than murder!

LADY MACBETH: My worthy lord,
Your noble friends are waiting for you.

MACBETH: Oh! I almost forgot.
Do not wonder at me, my worthy friends.
I have a strange illness, which is nothing
To those who know me.
Come, love and health to you all!
Give me some wine, a full glass.
I drink to the joy of the whole table, and to
Our dear friend Banquo, whom we miss.
We drink to all and to him!

LORDS: To the joy of all!

*(The **ghost** enters again.)*

MACBETH *(to the ghost)*: Quit my sight!
Let the earth hide you! Your bones have
No marrow. Your blood is cold.
Those glaring eyes cannot see!

LADY MACBETH: Think of this, good lords,
As just a sad ailment. It's no more.
Don't let it spoil your pleasure.

MACBETH *(to the ghost)*: What a man dares,

I dare. Approach like a rugged Russian bear,
An armored rhinoceros, or a wild tiger!
Take any shape but your own, and my nerves
Shall never tremble. Or be alive again, and
Dare me to a fight with your sword.
If I tremble at all, call me a little girl's doll.
Go away, horrible mocking shadow!

*(The **ghost** disappears.)*

Why, now it is gone.
I am myself again. Please, be seated, all.

LADY MACBETH: You've chased away the cheer
And ruined the whole evening
With your amazing disorder!

MACBETH: Can such things appear,
And overcome us like a summer's cloud,
Without our special wonder? You make me
A stranger to myself when I think
You can behold such sights,
And keep the natural ruby of your cheeks,
When mine are white with fear.

ROSS: What sights, my lord?

LADY MACBETH: Please, do not speak to him.
He grows worse and worse.
Questions enrage him. And so, good night.
Do not leave in the order of your ranks,
But all go at once.

LENNOX: Good night. May better health
Come to his majesty!

51

LADY MACBETH: A kind good night to all!

*(**Lords** and **attendants** exit.)*

MACBETH: The ghost wants revenge, I know.
Blood will be repaid in blood.
What time is it?

LADY MACBETH: Almost midnight.

MACBETH: What do you say to the fact that
Macduff did not come to the coronation
And ignored this banquet as well?

LADY MACBETH: Did he send a messenger?

MACBETH: No, he didn't.
But I will send one to him tomorrow.
I have at least one spy among the servants
At each nobleman's house,
So I know what Macduff has been saying.
Tomorrow I will visit the weird sisters,
For now I am determined to know,
By the worst methods, the worst news.
For my own good, all other matters
Must come second. I am standing so deep
In blood now that, if it were a river,
I would have to cross it. At this point,
It is easier to move on than to wade back.
I have strange ideas in my head,
And I must act upon them.

LADY MACBETH: You need some sleep.

MACBETH: Come, we'll sleep then.

My strange vision of the ghost
Is the fear of a beginner in evil.
We are yet but young in deed.

*(**They** exit.)*

| Scene 5 |

*(**Lennox** and **another lord** enter a room in the palace.)*

LENNOX: Strange things have been happening.
  The gracious Duncan visited Macbeth,
  And soon was dead.
  Then the brave Banquo, out walking late,
  Was killed by his son Fleance, who fled—
    Or so Macbeth would have us believe.
  Who cannot help thinking how monstrous
  It was for Malcolm and Donalbain
  To kill their gracious father? A terrible thing!
  How it grieved Macbeth! Didn't he kill
  The two guards in an angry rage? Anyone
  Could see that they had been
  Drinking too much and were sound asleep.
  Wasn't that a noble act of Macbeth's?
  Yes, and wise, too—for it would have
    angered
  Any heart alive to hear the guards deny it.
  I wonder what Macbeth would do if he had

Duncan's sons and Fleance locked up.
I'm sure they'd soon see the punishment for
Killing a father. But, enough about that!
I hear Macduff lives in disgrace, too,
For failing to come to the tyrant's feast.
Sir, can you tell me where Macduff is now?

LORD: Malcolm, Duncan's son,
From whom Macbeth stole the crown,
Is in England now, at King Edward's court.
Macduff has gone to England, too,
To help raise an army against Macbeth,
Who wants war with England.
If Malcolm and Macduff are successful,
We may again live in peace someday,
Without fear of bloody knives at banquets.

LENNOX: May a holy angel fly to the court
Of England to help Macduff.
May a swift blessing soon return
To our suffering country!

LORD: I'll send my prayers with him.

*(**Both** exit.)*

Act 4

| Scene 1 |

*(A dark cave with a cauldron boiling in the middle. Thunder sounds. The **three witches** enter.)*

WITCH 1: Round about the cauldron go;
Into the pot these things we'll throw.

ALL: Double, double, toil and trouble.
Fire, burn, and cauldron, bubble.

WITCH 2: From the swamp came this snake.
In the cauldron boil and bake.
Eye of newt and toe of frog,
Wool of bat and tongue of dog,
For a charm of powerful trouble,
Broth of evil, boil and bubble.

ALL: Double, double, toil and trouble,
Fire, burn, and cauldron, bubble.

WITCH 3: Tooth of wolf, and dragon's scale,
Witch's mummy, eye and nail,
Add a little, then a lot,
All these go into the pot.

ALL: Double, double, toil and trouble.
Fire, burn, and cauldron, bubble.

WITCH 2: Cool it with a baboon's blood,
Then the charm is firm and good.

WITCH 3: By the prickling in my thumbs,
Something wicked this way comes.
Open, locks, whoever knocks!

*(**Macbeth** enters.)*

MACBETH: You secret, midnight hags!
What is it you do?

ALL: A deed without a name.

MACBETH: I want to ask you some questions.

WITCH 1: Us or our masters?

MACBETH: Call them. Let me see them.

WITCH 1: Pour in sow's blood, that has eaten
Her nine piglets. And some sweat

Taken from a murderer's gallows.
Throw these into the flame.

ALL: Come, high or low;
To ourselves, yourself show!

*(Thunder sounds. **Vision 1**, a head wearing armor, appears, rising out of the cauldron.)*

VISION 1: Macbeth! Macbeth! Macbeth!
Beware Macduff. Beware the thane
of Fife.
I go. I've said enough.

*(**Vision 1** disappears into the cauldron.)*

WITCH 1: He will not appear again.
Here's another, more powerful than
the first.

*(Thunder sounds. **Vision 2**, a bloody child, appears, rising out of the cauldron.)*

VISION 2: Be strong, bold, and firm.
Laugh to scorn the power of man, for
None of woman born shall harm Macbeth!

*(**Vision 2** disappears into the cauldron.)*

MACBETH: Then live, Macduff!
Why should I fear you? But,
Just to be sure, I'll make a deal with fate—
You shall *not* live, so I may put
All my pale-hearted fear to rest,
And sleep in spite of thunder.

*(Thunder sounds. **Vision 3**, a crowned child, appears, holding a tree and rising out of the cauldron.)*

MACBETH: What is this, rising like a king's son,
Wearing on his baby brow the crown
And signs of royalty?

ALL: Listen, but do not speak to it.

VISION 3: Be brave as a lion, and be proud.
Do not worry about your enemies.
Macbeth shall never be beaten until
Birnam Wood comes to Dunsinane Hill
And fights against him.

*(**Vision 3** disappears into the cauldron.)*

MACBETH: That will never be!
Who can force a forest to fight a war?
Sweet words, good! Rebel armies will
Not rise until the wood of Birnam rises.
Royal Macbeth shall live as long
As nature intended. Yet my heart throbs
To know one thing: Tell me if Banquo's sons
Shall ever reign in this kingdom.

ALL: Seek to know no more.

MACBETH: I must know! Deny me this,
And an eternal curse fall on you!
Tell me—

ALL: Show his eyes, and grieve his heart.
Come like shadows, then depart!

*(A show of **eight kings** and **Banquo**, the last, rises from the cauldron holding a mirror.)*

MACBETH *(speaking to each king in turn)***:**
You are too much like the spirit of Banquo!
Go back down! Your crown burns my eyes!
And your hair is golden, like the first one.
A third is like the others. Filthy hags!
Why do you show me this? A fourth!
What, will the line never end?
Another yet! A seventh! I'll see no more!
And yet the eighth appears, with a mirror
That shows me many more. Horrible sight!
Now I see, it is true. They will *all* be kings!
The blood-spattered Banquo smiles at me,
And points at them, as if to say they are his.
What! Is this so?

WITCH 1: Yes, sir, all this is so. But why
Does Macbeth stand here so amazed?
Come, sisters, let's take our leave.
I'll charm the air to give a sound,
While you perform your dances round,
So this great king may kindly say,
We answered his questions on this day.

*(Music. The **witches** dance and then vanish.)*

MACBETH: Where are they? Gone?
Let this evil hour be accursed!
I hear someone coming.
Come in, whoever is out there!

*(**Lennox** enters.)*

LENNOX: What is your grace's will?

MACBETH: Did you see the weird sisters?

LENNOX: No, my lord.

MACBETH: Did they not pass by you?

LENNOX: No, indeed, my lord.

MACBETH: I heard the galloping of a horse.
    Who was it that came by?

LENNOX: A few of us came to tell you
    That Macduff has fled to England.

MACBETH: Fled to England!

LENNOX: Yes, my good lord.

MACBETH *(aside)***:** If I hadn't come here,
    I might have had time to stop Macduff.
    From now on, as soon as I think about
    Doing something, I will do it.
    I will surprise Macduff's castle and
    Give the edge of the sword to his wife,
    His babes, and all unlucky relatives who
    Might happen to be there.
    I will not boast about it like a fool.
    This deed I'll do before my anger cools.
    *(to Lennox)***:** Where are these gentlemen?
    Come, bring me where they are.

*(**All** exit.)*

| Scene 2 |

*(Fife. A room in Macduff's castle. **Lady Macduff, her son**, and **Ross** enter.)*

LADY MACDUFF: What had he done,
  To make him leave Scotland?

ROSS: You must have patience, madam.

LADY MACDUFF: He had none.
  His flight was madness. His action
  Makes him look like a traitor.

ROSS: You do not know whether he left
  Out of wisdom or of fear.

LADY MACDUFF: Wisdom! To leave his wife,
  To leave his babes, his castle, and his title,
  In a place from which he himself does fly?
  He loves us not. He lacks natural feelings.
  Even the wren, the smallest of birds,
  Will fight the owl to protect her babies.
  He is all fear and no love, running away
  Against all reason.

ROSS: My dear cousin, I beg you, calm down.
  Your husband is noble, wise, and careful.
  He best knows the problems of the day.
  I dare not speak further.
  But the times are cruel when we are accused
  Of being traitors without knowing why!
  We float upon a wild and violent sea,

61

Moving each way the waves take us.
I must leave, but I'll soon return.
Blessings on you, my pretty cousin!

*(**Ross** exits.)*

LADY MACDUFF: My son, your father's dead.
What will you do now? How will you live?

SON: As birds do, Mother.

LADY MACDUFF: What, on worms and flies?

SON: No, with whatever I can get, as they do.

LADY MACDUFF: Poor bird! Wouldn't you fear
The traps, the hunter, or the snares?

SON: Why should I, Mother?
Poor birds are not hunted.
My father is not dead, though you say so.

LADY MACDUFF: Yes, he is dead.
What will you do for a father?

SON: No, what will you do for a husband?

LADY MACDUFF: I can buy 20 at any market.

SON: Then you'll buy them to sell again.

LADY MACDUFF: You speak with such wit!

SON: Was my father a traitor, Mother?

LADY MACDUFF: Yes, he was.

SON: What is a traitor?

LADY MACDUFF: One who swears and lies.

SON: And do all traitors do so?

LADY MACDUFF: Everyone that does so
　　Is a traitor, and must be hanged.

SON: Must all who swear and lie be hanged?

LADY MACDUFF: Every one.

SON: Who must hang them?

LADY MACDUFF: Why, the honest men.

SON: Then the liars and swearers are fools,
　　For there are enough of them
　　To beat the honest men and hang them all.

LADY MACDUFF: God help you, poor monkey!
　　But what will you do for a father?

SON: If he were dead, you'd weep for him.
　　If you don't weep for him, it's a good sign
　　That I will quickly have a new father.

LADY MACDUFF: How you talk!

*(A **messenger** enters.)*

MESSENGER: Bless you, fair lady! You don't
　　Know me, but I know who you are.
　　You must get away from here.
　　Run, with your little ones!
　　There are those who mean to do you harm.
　　Heaven help you! I dare stay here no longer.

*(**Messenger** exits.)*

LADY MACDUFF: Where should I go?
　　I have done no harm. But I remember now

I am in this earthly world. To do harm is
Often praiseworthy. To do good can be
Dangerous folly. Why, then, alas,
Do I put up that womanly defense,
To say I have done no harm?

*(**Murderers** enter.)*

Who are you?

MURDERER 1: Where is your husband?

LADY MACDUFF: I hope he is in no place so bad
   Where such as you may find him.

MURDERER 1: He's a traitor.

SON: You lie, you shaggy-haired villain!

MURDERER 1 *(stabbing him)***:** What, you egg!
   You son of a traitor!

SON: He has killed me, Mother.
   Run away, I pray you!

*(**Son** dies. **Lady Macduff** exits, crying "Murder!"
Murderers exit, following her.)*

| Scene 3 |

*(England. Before the king's palace. **Malcolm** and
Macduff enter.)*

MALCOLM: Let us seek out some lonely shade
   And weep there until our tears are gone.

MACDUFF: Let us instead pick up our swords,
And march to our downfallen country.
Each new morning, new widows howl,
New orphans cry, new sorrows hit heaven.
Heaven echoes in sympathy with Scotland,
Yelling out the same cries of sorrow.

MALCOLM: I'll cry for what is happening,
But what I can change, I will.
You may speak the truth.
You once loved this tyrant,
Whose name blisters our tongues.
He has not touched you yet. That makes me
Think that you might still be loyal to him.
Perhaps you plan to win favors from him
By betraying me—a poor, innocent lamb—
To appease an angry god.

MACDUFF: I am not treacherous!

MALCOLM: But Macbeth is.
A good and virtuous nature might act
Dishonorably at a king's command.
But I beg your pardon for these thoughts.
What you are, my thoughts cannot change.

MACDUFF: I have lost my hopes.

MALCOLM: I have wondered why you left your
Wife and child, those strong knots of love,
Without saying goodbye. Still, I have no
Reason to mistrust you. You may be
Just and true, no matter what I fear.

MACDUFF: Bleed, bleed, poor country!
　Great tyranny! Farewell, my lord.
　I would not be the villain that you suspect
　For all the space in the tyrant's grasp!

MALCOLM: Do not be offended.
　I am not in absolute fear of you.
　Our country suffers under Macbeth.
　Each day a gash is added to her wounds.
　I will find support for my cause.
　In fact, the King of England has offered
　Many thousands to help me. But, for all this,
　When I shall tread upon the tyrant's head, or
　Wear it on my sword, still my poor country
　Will have more troubles than it had before.
　It may suffer more, in more ways than ever,
　By him who wears the crown after Macbeth.

MACDUFF: Who would he be?

MALCOLM: I mean myself. I know my faults.
　When others see them, evil Macbeth
　Will look as pure as snow.
　The state will regard him as a lamb,
　Compared to my endless harms.

MACDUFF: Nobody could top Macbeth in evils!

MALCOLM: I grant that he is brutal, lustful,
　Greedy, false, deceitful, and violent.
　He smacks of every sin that has a name.
　But there's no bottom—none—to *my* evil.
　Your wives, your daughters, your maids, and

Your old women could not satisfy my lust.
Better Macbeth than such a one to reign.

MACDUFF: Such lust is not natural.
It has been the cause of great unhappiness
And the fall of many kings. But fear not
To take what is yours. You could enjoy
The company of many willing women.

MALCOLM: That is not my only failing.
I am also greedy. If I were king,
I would take the nobles' lands,
Demand this one's jewels, that one's house.
The more I got, the more I would want.
Eventually, I'd create unfair quarrels
With the good and loyal,
Destroying them for wealth.

MACDUFF: This greed is worse than young lust.
It has been the sword that killed many kings.
Yet do not fear. Scotland has much wealth
To satisfy you without harming anyone.
All your faults can be tolerated,
Considering your virtues.

MALCOLM: But I have none. The graces that are
Becoming to a king—justice, honesty,
Moderation, stability, generosity, mercy,
Humility, devotion, patience, courage—
I have none of them. Instead, I lean
Toward crime, showing it in many ways.
No, if I had power, I would upset the
Universal peace, confuse all unity on earth.

MACDUFF: Oh, Scotland, Scotland!

MALCOLM: If such a one is fit to rule, speak.
I am as I have spoken.

MACDUFF: Fit to rule? No, not to live!
Oh, miserable nation!
With a bloodthirsty tyrant on the throne,
When shall you see healthy days again,
If the rightful heir is not fit to rule?
Malcolm, your royal father, Duncan,
Was a most sainted king. The queen who
Was your mother lived a life of daily prayer.
Farewell! These evils that you confess
Have banished me from Scotland.
Oh, my country! Your hope ends here!

MALCOLM: Macduff, your noble passion
For Scotland has shown me your honor
And proven to me that you are trustworthy.
The evil Macbeth has often tried to win me
Into his power by offers of women,
Power, and riches—but you did not.
I now assure you that the vices I named
Are strangers to me. I have never even
Been with a woman. I have never lied.
I have hardly even wanted what was mine.
At no time have I broken my faith,
Nor betrayed anyone.
I delight no less in truth than in life.
My first lie was to tell you that I was evil.

What I truly am is this: I am yours,
And my poor country's, to command.
All I want is to serve my country well.
In fact, before you got here, an
English general, with 10,000 warlike men,
Ready for battle, was leaving for Scotland.
We'll go together! But why are you silent?

MACDUFF: Such welcome and unwelcome news
At once! It's hard to take it all in.
See, who comes here?

MALCOLM: I do not recognize him.

(Ross enters.)

MACDUFF: Gentle cousin, welcome to England.

MALCOLM: I know him now! I've been away
From Scotland too long. May that soon end!

ROSS: Sir, may it be so.

MACDUFF: Is Scotland still the same?

ROSS: Alas, poor country—
Almost afraid to know itself! It cannot
Now be called our mother, but our grave.
Sighs, groans, and shrieks tear the air.
Violence and sorrow are everywhere.
The bell for the dead rings so often that
No one even asks who has died.
Good men's lives end
Before the flowers in their caps wither.
They die before they have time to get sick.

69

MALCOLM: What's the newest grief?

ROSS: Hour-long news is already old.
　　Each minute brings a new one.

MACDUFF: How is my wife?

ROSS: Why, well and at peace.

MACDUFF: And all my children?

ROSS: They were at peace when I left them.

MACDUFF: Don't be so stingy with your words!
　　What's happening in Scotland?

ROSS: I've heard that many worthy Scots
　　Have taken up arms against the tyrant.
　　I believe this rumor is true, because I saw
　　The tyrant's soldiers out marching.
　　We need help now.
　　(to Malcolm): If only you were in Scotland,
　　Soldiers would follow you. Even
　　Women would fight to get rid of Macbeth.

MALCOLM: Tell them that we are coming.
　　The King of England has lent us
　　Good Siward and 10,000 men.
　　An older and better soldier
　　Cannot be found anywhere.

ROSS: I wish I had good news of my own.
　　But my words should be howled out
　　In the desert air, where no one would hear.

MACDUFF: What is your news?
　　The general cause? Or is it a private grief

For one person alone?

ROSS: Every honest mind shares in the woe,
Though the main part is about you alone.

MACDUFF: If it concerns me, you must tell me.
Quickly, let me have it!

ROSS: Do not let your ears hate my tongue,
For I shall fill them with the heaviest sound
That they have ever heard.

MACDUFF: I can guess at what you will say.

ROSS: Your castle was surprised,
Your wife and babes savagely slaughtered.
I cannot tell you anymore details,
For I fear it would kill you.

MALCOLM: Merciful heaven! Macduff,
Give words to your sorrow! The grief
That does not speak whispers to the heart
And tells it to break.

MACDUFF: My children, too?

ROSS: Wife, children, servants—
All that could be found.

MACDUFF: And I had to be away!
My wife was killed, too?

ROSS: I have said so.

MALCOLM: Be comforted.
Let's cure this deadly grief with revenge.

MACDUFF: But Macbeth has no children.

All my pretty ones? Did you say all? *All?*
My pretty children and their mother
At one fell swoop?

MALCOLM: Take revenge for this like a man.

MACDUFF: I must also feel it as a man.
I cannot stop thinking about those
Who were most precious to me.
Did heaven look on, and not help them?
They were killed because of me—
Not for their faults, but for mine.
May heaven rest them now!

MALCOLM: Let this sharpen your sword.
Turn your grief into anger.
Blunt not your heart—enrage it!

MACDUFF: Gentle heavens, without delay
Bring me face to face
With this fiend of Scotland.
Set him within my sword's length.
If he escapes, may heaven forgive him!

MALCOLM: That's the right idea! Come, let's go
to the king. The army is ready.
All we need is his permission to leave.
Macbeth is like fruit ripe on the tree,
Ready for shaking.
Receive what cheer you may;
The night is long that never finds the day.

*(**All** exit.)*

Act 5

| Scene 1 |

*(Dunsinane. A room in the castle. A **doctor** and a **gentlewoman** enter.)*

GENTLEWOMAN: Since his majesty went into the field with the army, I have seen her do it many times. She rises from bed, takes out a paper, folds it, writes on it, and reads it. Then she seals it and again returns to bed. And she does all this while she is fast asleep.

DOCTOR: Has she said anything?

GENTLEWOMAN: Many things, sir, which I would rather not report.

DOCTOR: You may tell me. In fact, you should.

GENTLEWOMAN: No. I have no witness to back me up. Look—here she comes!

*(**Lady Macbeth** enters, carrying a candle.)*

That is just how she looks. See, she's fast asleep. Watch her. Stand close.

DOCTOR: How did she get that candle?

GENTLEWOMAN: By her command, she always has light by her bedside.

DOCTOR: Look, her eyes are open!

GENTLEWOMAN: Yes, but she sees nothing.

DOCTOR: Watch how she rubs her hands!

GENTLEWOMAN: Yes, she seems to be washing her hands. I have seen her do this for 15 minutes at a time.

LADY MACBETH: Still, here's a spot.

DOCTOR: Listen, she speaks! I will write down what comes from her, to remember it better.

LADY MACBETH: Out, damned spot! Out, I say! One o'clock, two o'clock. Why, then, it's time to do it. My lord, we need not fear who knows it, for nobody can challenge our power now. Yet who would have thought the old man would have had so much blood in him?

DOCTOR: Do you hear that?

LADY MACBETH: The Thane of Fife had a wife. Where is she now? What, will these hands never be clean? No more of that, my lord, no more of that. You'll ruin everything with your startled movements.

DOCTOR *(to Lady Macbeth)***:** You seem to know things you should not know.

LADY MACBETH *(her hand to her nose)***:** Here's the smell of the blood still. *(sighing)***:** All the perfumes of Arabia will not sweeten this little hand.

DOCTOR: What a groan! Her heart is heavy.

GENTLEWOMAN: I would not have such a heart in my body for anything!

DOCTOR: This disease is beyond my practice.

LADY MACBETH: Wash your hands. Do not look so pale. I tell you—Banquo's buried! He cannot return from his grave. To bed! Oh! There's knocking at the gate. Come, come? Give me your hand. What's done cannot be undone. To bed, to bed, to bed.

*(**Lady Macbeth** exits.)*

DOCTOR: Will she go to bed now?

GENTLEWOMAN: Right away.

DOCTOR: I have heard people whispering
    About evil deeds done here.
    She needs divine help—not mine!
    Look after her. And now, good night.
    What I have seen has amazed my sight.
    I think, but I dare not speak.

*(**Both** exit.)*

| Scene 2 |

*(The country near Dunsinane. Drums sound. Enter
Menteith, Caithness, Angus, Lennox, and **soldiers**.)*

MENTEITH: The English army is near,
    Led by Malcolm, Siward, and Macduff.
    Desire for revenge burns in them.
    Their dear causes are so just
    That even a dead man would rise to help!

ANGUS: We'll meet them near Birnam Wood.
    That is the way they are coming.

CAITHNESS: Is Donalbain with his brother?

LENNOX: For certain, sir, he is not. I have
    A list of all the men. There is Siward's
    Son, along with many beardless youth
    Who claim they are old enough to fight.

MENTEITH: What is the tyrant Macbeth doing?

CAITHNESS: Protecting his castle, Dunsinane.
Some say he's mad. Others, who
Hate him less, call it brave fury.

ANGUS: Now he feels his secret murders
Sticking on his hands!
Now small revolts challenge him daily.
Those he commands move only because
He commands it—not because of their
love for him.
His title now hangs loose about him,
Like a giant's robe on a dwarfish thief.

CAITHNESS: Well, let's march on
To give obedience where it is truly owed.
We will soon meet Malcolm, the medicine
That will cure Scotland and heal us all.

LENNOX: Yes, let's march on to Birnam Wood.

(*All* exit, marching.)

| Scene 3 |

(*Dunsinane. A room in the castle. **Macbeth,** the
doctor, and **attendants** enter.*)

MACBETH: Bring me no more reports.
Until Birnam Wood moves to Dunsinane,
I have nothing to fear. What is Malcolm?

Was he not born of woman? The spirits
That know the future have told me this:
"No man of woman born shall harm
  Macbeth."

*(A **servant** enters.)*

What do you want, you pale-faced goose?

SERVANT: There are 10,000—

MACBETH: Geese, villain?

SERVANT: Soldiers, sir.

MACBETH: Why does that scare you,
  You lily-livered boy? What soldiers, fool?

SERVANT: The English force, your majesty.

MACBETH: Take your face away from here!

*(**Servant** exits.)*

I am sick at heart. This battle will either
Secure my throne or overthrow me.
I have lived long enough. My youth is over.
That which should accompany old age,
Such as honor, love, obedience, friends,
I must not expect to have. Instead,
I have men who obey me out of fear.
  (to the doctor): How is your patient, Doctor?

DOCTOR: Her body is well enough, my lord.
But her mind is troubled with visions
That keep her from her rest.

MACBETH: Cure her of that.
Can you not minister to a sick mind,
Pluck from the memory a deep sorrow, and
Erase the written troubles of the brain?
Clean out the dangerous stuff
That weighs upon her heart
With some sweet medicine of forgetting!

DOCTOR: In cases like this, the patient
Must minister to himself.

MACBETH: Throw medicine to the dogs!
I'll have none of it.
Doctor, the thanes are all leaving me.
If you can find the disease that is troubling
My land, bring her back to a healthy state.

DOCTOR: My good lord, I wish I could.

MACBETH: I will not fear death and pain;
Until Birnam Wood comes to Dunsinane.

(All exit except the doctor.)

DOCTOR: If I were away from Dunsinane,
Free and clear,
No amount of profit could bring me here.

(Doctor exits.)

| Scene 4 |

*(Country near Birnam Wood. Drums sound. **Malcolm**, old **Siward** and **his son**, **Macduff**, **Menteith**, **Angus**, **Caithness**, **Lennox**, **Ross**, and **soldiers** march up.)*

SIWARD: What wood is this before us?

MENTEITH: The wood of Birnam.

MALCOLM: Let every soldier cut down a branch
And carry it before him. That way, we will
Hide our great numbers, and cause the spies
To err in reporting back to Macbeth.

SOLDIERS: It shall be done.

SIWARD: We hear that Macbeth is still in
Dunsinane, waiting there for us.

MALCOLM: It's his main hope, for he knows
That his men can more easily desert him
On the battlefield than in the castle.
None serve him but those who are forced to.
Their hearts are somewhere else.

MACDUFF: Let us think only of the battle ahead.
Good soldiers are not distracted by rumors.

SIWARD: The time comes that will let us know
What we shall have, and what we shall owe.
Guessing the outcome reveals our hopes,
The issues will be decided by strokes.
So may the battle begin.

*(**All** exit, marching.)*

| Scene 5 |

*(Dunsinane, within the castle. **Macbeth**, **Seyton**, and **soldiers** enter.)*

MACBETH: Hang our flags on the outer walls.
　　Our castle's strength will laugh at them.
　　Here let them lie until starvation and fever
　　Eat them up. If they had not been reinforced
　　With soldiers who deserted us,
　　We might have been able to meet them
　　Beard to beard, and beat them back home.

(Wailing cries are heard from within.)
　　What is that noise?

SEYTON: It is the cry of women, my good lord.

*(**Seyton** exits.)*

MACBETH: I have almost forgotten
　　The taste of fears. In the past, my senses
　　Would have cooled to hear a night shriek,
　　And my hair would have stood on end.
　　But I've become so accustomed to horror
　　That not even such a shriek startles me.

*(**Seyton** enters again.)*
　　What was that cry all about?

SEYTON: The queen, my lord, is dead.

MACBETH: She should have died later—when
　　There would have been time for mourning.

Tomorrow, and tomorrow, and tomorrow,
Creeps on this petty pace from day to day,
To the last syllable of recorded time;
And all our yesterdays have lighted fools
The way to dusty death. Out, out, brief
  candle!
Life's but a walking shadow, a poor player
That struts and frets his hour upon the stage
And then is heard no more. It is a tale
Told by an idiot, full of sound and fury,
Signifying nothing.

*(A **messenger** enters.)*

You came to say something. Say it quickly.

MESSENGER: As I stood my watch upon the hill,
I looked toward Birnam. It seemed
The wood had begun to move!

MACBETH: If you are lying, you shall be hanged
Upon the nearest tree until you starve.
If your words are true,
I do not care if you do the same to me.
Now I doubt the words of the Vision
That makes lies sound like truth:
"Macbeth shall never be beaten until
Birnam Wood comes to Dunsinane Hill."
You say a wood moves toward Dunsinane?
Every man take up arms! Prepare to fight!
Ring the alarms! Blow, wind! Come, attack!
At least we'll die with armor on our back.

*(**All** exit.)*

| Scene 6 |

*(A plain before the castle. Drums sound. **Malcolm, old Siward, Macduff**, and their **army** enter, carrying tree branches.)*

MALCOLM: Now we are near enough.
Throw down your leafy screens
And show who you are.
*(to old Siward)***:** You, worthy uncle,
  shall lead our first battle,
Along with my cousin, your noble son.
Brave Macduff and I shall lead the others.

SIWARD: Fare you well.
If we find the tyrant's army tonight,
Let us be beaten, if we fail to fight.

MACDUFF: Make all our trumpets speak—
Give them the breath
To loudly sing of blood and death.

*(**All** exit.)*

| Scene 7 |

*(Another part of the plain. **Macbeth** enters.)*

MACBETH: I am like a bear tied to a stake.
I cannot run, but, bearlike, I must fight.
Who is he that was not born of woman?
He is the one I must fear—or nobody.

*(**Young Siward** enters.)*

YOUNG SIWARD: What is your name?

MACBETH: My name's Macbeth.

YOUNG SIWARD: The devil himself could not
Say a name more hateful to my ear.

MACBETH: No, nor more fearful.

YOUNG SIWARD: You lie, hated tyrant!
With my sword, I'll prove it.

(They fight, and young Siward is killed.)

MACBETH: You were born of woman!
At swords I smile and all weapons scorn,
When taken up by man of woman born.

*(**Macbeth** exits. Young Siward's body is removed from
the stage. **Macduff** enters.)*

MACDUFF: Tyrant, show your face!
If you are killed by someone other than me,
The ghosts of my wife and children will
Haunt me forever. I will not strike your
Wretched soldiers, who fight for money.
Either it's you, Macbeth,
Or I shall put my sword away unused.
Judging by all the noise, you should be close.
Let me find him, Fortune! I beg for no more.

*(**Macduff** exits. **Malcolm** and **old Siward** enter.)*

SIWARD: This way, my lord.
The castle has been surrendered.

The noble thanes are winning the war!
Victory soon declares itself yours.
There is little left to do.

MALCOLM: We have met with some foes
Who now fight on our side.

SIWARD: Enter, sir, the castle.

*(**All** exit.)*

| Scene 8 |

*(Another part of the field. **Macbeth** enters.)*

MACBETH: Why should I kill myself with my
Own sword, just because we are losing?
While I see live enemies,
The gashes would be better on them.

*(**Macduff** enters.)*

MACDUFF: Turn, you villain, turn!

MACBETH: Of all the men here,
I have avoided you. Get back, back!
My soul is too heavy
With your blood already.

MACDUFF: I have no words for you—
My voice is in my sword. You are
A bloodier villain than words can say!

(They fight.)

MACBETH: You are wasting your efforts.
It would be easier for you to cut the air
With your sword than to make me bleed!
Let your blade fall on men you can harm.
I live a charmed life, which will not yield
To a man born of woman.

MACDUFF: Despair of your charm!
Let the devil whom you still serve
Tell you this: Macduff was ripped
From his mother's womb early.
I was not born in the normal way.

MACBETH: Cursed be the tongue that says so,
For it has made my courage fail!
Those deceiving fiends are liars.
They fool us with double meanings.
I won't fight with you.

MACDUFF: Then give up, coward—
And live to be the sideshow of the time!
We'll have your picture painted on a pole,
As we do with our rarer monsters.
Under it we'll write, "Here is the tyrant."

MACBETH: I will not give up,
To kiss the ground at young Malcolm's feet,
And be taunted by the commoners.
So Birnam Wood has come to Dunsinane,
And you were not born of a woman!
Still I will fight to the last. Before my body,

I hold my warlike shield. Fight on, Macduff,
And cursed be he who first cries, "Enough!"

*(**They** exit, fighting. Drums sound, and **Malcolm, old Siward, Ross, Lennox, Angus, Caithness, Menteith,** and **soldiers** enter.)*

MALCOLM: Oh, that our missing friends
Had arrived here safely!

SIWARD: Some must die in battle. And yet,
It looks as if we lost very few soldiers.

MALCOLM: Macduff is missing, and your son.

ROSS: Your son, my lord, was killed in battle.
He lived only until he was a man,
Then like a man he died.

SIWARD: You say he is dead?

SERVANT: Yes. Your reason for sorrow
Must not be measured by his worth,
For then it would have no end.

SIWARD: Were his wounds on the front?

ROSS: Yes, on the front of his body.

SIWARD: Why, then, he died bravely,
Facing his enemy.
If I had as many sons as I have hairs,
I would not wish them a fairer death.
And so, God be with him.

*(**Macduff** enters, carrying Macbeth's head.)*

MACDUFF *(to Malcolm)*: Hail, king! See this,
The tyrant's cursed head. We are now
free.
Hail, King of Scotland!
ALL: Hail, King of Scotland!

(Trumpets sound.)

MALCOLM: I shall not waste any time before
Rewarding all of you for your efforts today.
My thanes and kinsmen, from this day on,
You are earls, the first named in Scotland.
We shall soon call our exiled friends home,
And bring to trial the cruel ministers
Of this dead butcher and his fiendish queen,
Who, they say, took her own life.
So, thanks to all of you whom
We invite to see us crowned at Scone.

*(Trumpets sound. **All** exit.)*